Big Book of

Princess Stories

Miles Kelly

First published in 2015 by Miles Kelly Publishing Ltd
Harding's Barn, Bardfield End Green, Thaxted, Essex, CM6 3PX, UK

Copyright © Miles Kelly Publishing Ltd 2015

2 4 6 8 10 9 7 5 3 1

Publishing Director Belinda Gallagher
Creative Director Jo Cowan
Editorial Director Rosie Neave
Senior Editor Claire Philip
Design Manager Joe Jones
Production Elizabeth Collins, Caroline Kelly
Reprographics Stephan Davis, Jennifer Cozens, Thom Allaway

ISBN 978-1-78209-820-1

Printed in China

British Library Cataloguing-in-Publication Data
A catalogue record for this book is available from the British Library

ACKNOWLEDGEMENTS
The publishers would like to thank the following artists who have contributed to this book:
Advocate Art: Giuliana Gregori (Cinderella) and Natalia Moore (Snow White and the Seven Dwarfs)
The Bright Agency: Rosie Butcher (Sleeping Beauty) and Charlotte Cooke (The Princess and the Pea)

Made with paper from a sustainable forest

www.mileskelly.net
info@mileskelly.net

Cinderella

Once apon a time, there was a young girl called Cinderella. She lived with her mean stepmother and two stepsisters.

4

She worked hard all day long
and at night she slept by the
fireside, in the ashes.

5

One day, a letter arrived from the palace. The prince was holding a ball, and everyone was invited. Cinderella's stepmother said to her, "You cannot go. You must stay here and mind the fires."

On the day of the ball, Cinderella
helped her stepsisters get ready.
"Have fun at home!" they teased. 7

Poor Cinderella watched the carriage drive away, then sat down, almost in tears.

"How I wish I could go to the ball," she said.

Suddenly, a kind-looking
old lady appeared! She had
glittery wings and a wand.
"Hello Cinderella," she said.

"I'm your fairy godmother.
I will grant you your wish."

"You shall go
to the ball!"

Cinderella's fairy godmother smiled and said, "First we need a way to get you to the palace. Fetch the largest pumpkin from the vegetable patch!"

She waved her wand
and the pumpkin became
a carriage!

11

"Now you need some horses and a driver to take you to the palace!" said the fairy godmother.

12

And in two flicks of her wand,
four mice became four horses,
and a rat became a coachman.

Now for the most important part, said Cinderella's fairy godmother, "your gown."

She twirled her wand, and when Cinderella looked down she was wearing a beautiful dress, and sparkling glass slippers.

14

Cinderella's fairy godmother said
she was ready for the ball, but that she
must be home by midnight. "The spell will
end as the clock strikes twelve!" 15

When Cinderella arrived at the palace everyone turned to look at her. "Who is that beautiful young lady?" they asked.

Nobody recognized her, not even her stepsisters.

The prince danced with Cinderella all evening. She was enjoying herself so much that she didn't notice the time.

Suddenly the clock began to strike twelve! Cinderella ran from the palace but in her haste she lost one of her *glass slippers!*

When Cinderella returned to her carriage the spell had broken. She ran home quickly to make sure she was back before her stepsisters.

The prince, meanwhile, could not forget Cinderella. He had fallen in love and declared that he would marry the owner of the glass slipper.

He visited every house in the land,
but had no luck. Finally, he arrived
at Cinderella's house.

"This glass slipper belongs to the girl I danced with at the ball," the prince said, "I must find her."

Cinderella's stepsisters invited the prince inside, then they tried to force their big feet into the slipper, but with no luck!

The prince asked if
there were any other
young ladies at the house.
"Of course not," said the
stepsisters.

23

Just then, Cinderella stepped into the room, but
before she could speak her stepmother said,
"No, not her, she works in the kitchen –
she didn't go to the ball."

24

But the prince asked Cinderella
to sit down on the chair. She
placed her foot in the glass
slipper and it fitted perfectly!

Everyone was amazed!

Suddenly, the prince recognized Cinderella as the girl from the ball, and he was overjoyed! "I have found my bride at last," he cried. "Will you marry me?"

Cinderella said yes, and they lived happily ever after.

Sleeping Beauty

Once upon a time a
beautiful baby girl was
born to a king and queen.
They had wanted a child
for a long time, so they
were very happy.

The proud king soon began
organizing a christening feast
for his little princess.

All the king's family
and friends were
invited to the
christening.

They also asked the fairies to
come – all apart from one, who
was known for being mean.

On the big day the guests arrived, bringing lots of lovely gifts.

Congratulations your highness!

31

The fairies lined up to give the baby princess her presents.

They came forward one by one, casting spells of kindness, beauty and cleverness.

The last fairy was just about
to give her gift, when there was
a loud noise in the courtyard.

Crash!

33

Just then, the mean fairy who had not been invited burst in angrily, and said...

"When the princess is sixteen she shall touch a spindle and fall down dead!"

The queen collapsed into the king's arms in shock, but then the last fairy stepped forwards, "Wait!" she said.

"I can soften the curse a little," she said. "If the princess touches a spindle, she will not die."

"Instead, she will fall asleep for one hundred years. Only a prince shall be able to wake her...

with a single kiss."

The king gave out
an order for all the
spindles in the land
to be destroyed.

The princess
grew up into a
beautiful
young lady.

One day, while exploring
the castle, she came
across a door that she
hadn't seen before.

She opened it and found
steps leading up to a

mysterious tower.

The princess walked up the steps and into a dusty room. There she saw a woman, busy at a strange wheel with some thread.

"Hello, what are you doing?" asked the princess.

42

"I'm spinning, my dear," said the woman. The princess walked closer, and as she came to the spindle she reached out to touch it.

Whrrrrr whrrrr!

"Ouch!" the princess cried as her finger touched the spindle, and while the wicked fairy – for it was she – vanished, the princess fell down asleep.

At that moment the king and queen fell asleep on their thrones. The horses slept in their stables and the servants slipped into a slumber.

Days, weeks and then months went past,

and a large hedge of thorns grew around

the palace. Every year it became thicker,

until the palace was completely hidden.

Exactly one hundred years later, a prince was riding nearby. He could see the tips of a turret above the thorns. As he neared, the hedge parted, allowing him to pass through.

The prince eventually arrived at the palace and saw that everyone was sleeping.

He wondered why everything and everyone had been

frozen in time.

Finally, he came to the room where the princess was sleeping. She was so beautiful that he stooped down to give her a kiss. At that moment she opened her eyes and woke up.

It was love at first sight.

47

Everyone else in the castle also awoke.
At last the princess was reunited with her
mother and father. They were delighted!

The evil fairy's spell had been broken!

49

Sleeping Beauty and the prince were soon married, and they lived happily ever after!

Hip hip hooray!

The Princess and the Pea

Once upon a time, there was a handsome prince. He had everything he could wish for, but was quite lonely.

His parents, the king and queen, said that it might be time for him to look for a bride.

The prince thought this was a good idea, so he started his search for the perfect princess.

He held parties all over the kingdom, where he met plenty of perfectly pleasant girls who said they were princesses.

He also met some unpleasant princesses.
None, it seemed to him, were quite right.

But he carried
on looking...

The prince travelled to faraway lands, where royal families presented a host of suitable young ladies.

...or terrible table manners! Nowhere could he find a princess who lived up to his high standards.

So the prince returned to his palace, where he sat reading dusty books and getting

very glum.

One wintery night, there was the most terrible storm. The prince huddled close to the fire.

Just as everyone was going to bed there was a loud knocking at the door. The king, queen and prince went to see who it was.

Knock, knock!

There, absolutely dripping wet and covered in mud, stood a girl.

No one could have looked less like a princess, but that is exactly what the girl claimed to be.

61

Everyone thought it was very unlikely that the girl was a princess, but they invited her in and told her to take a seat by the fire.

The girl sat sipping a mug of warm milk and slowly dried off.

As the girl grew warmer
the prince noticed how rosy
her cheeks were, and how
pretty her laugh.

Woof
Woof!

The queen noticed the attention her son was paying to this mystery girl, and she decided to test whether or not she really was a princess.

65

The queen went to the
finest spare bedroom, and
gave orders to the maids.

She told them to take
all of the bedclothes
and the mattress
off the bed.

Then she placed

one single pea

on the middle of
the bedstead.

67

Next the maids piled dozens of mattresses, sheets, feather quilts and warm blankets on top of the pea.

Then the girl was shown
to her room and left
alone for the night.

In the morning, the queen
swept into the bedroom
and asked the girl,

"How did you sleep,
your highness?"

"I didn't sleep a wink all night," she replied.
"There was a great, hard lump in the middle of the bed. It was quite dreadful. I am sure I am black and blue all over!"

The queen was delighted. This meant that the girl really was a princess, for only a true princess could be as sensitive as that.

"She is a princess, after all!"

The prince proposed to the princess at once,
and they lived happily ever after.

The pea was placed in the royal museum, where it probably still is today.

THE PEA

Snow White
and the Seven Dwarfs

One winter's day, a baby girl was born to a king and queen. She was very pretty, with skin as white as snow and lips as red as blood.

She was named Snow White before her mother sadly died.

The king remarried, but his new queen was unkind and vain. She had a magic mirror, to which she would say,

"Mirror, mirror, on the wall, who is the fairest of them all?"

"You, O queen are the fairest of them all!"

Many years later, when Snow White was sixteen, the queen asked this same question, and the mirror replied:

"You, O queen, are very fair – but Snow White is now the fairest"

The queen was absolutely furious!
She ordered a huntsman to find
her stepdaughter and kill her.

The huntsman took
Snow White into the forest,
but he could not bring
himself to do the
wicked deed.

Instead, he told Snow White to flee, and went back to the queen, pretending he had carried out her wishes.

"Run away, Snow White, and never come back!"

Snow White ran and ran until evening began to fall, when she stumbled across a little cottage.

"I wonder if anyone is home," said Snow White.

She walked up the path and tried the door, and to Snow White's surprise it opened.

She went inside the cottage
to see if anyone was there.
Everything inside was very

small and neat.

Against the wall stood seven little beds. Snow White sank down on one and soon fell fast asleep.

85

Later that night the owners of the cottage came back – they were seven dwarfs, who had been mining in the mountains for jewels.

When Snow White awoke she explained to the dwarfs what had happened. They kindly said, "You are very welcome to stay here with us."

87

While the dwarfs went out to work Snow White looked after the cottage. Each day they warned her to beware of her stepmother.

"Apples for sale! Delicious, juicy, sweet apples!"

"No, thank you" said Snow White,
but the queen wouldn't take
no for an answer.

She cut off a piece from
the green half of the apple.
"Look, I will eat some first.
It is quite safe."

Snow White was hungry,
so she took the apple, taking a
bite from the rosy-red side.

Straight away
she fell down
as if dead!

The dwarfs put Snow White in a glass coffin. One day, a prince rode by. He knocked the coffin as he leant over it, and the

94 poisoned apple fell from Snow White's mouth. She awoke!

The prince took Snow White to his palace to recover, and they soon fell in love. The dwarfs were the guests of honour at the wedding!

Congratulations!

Meanwhile, the evil queen asked her mirror one last time, "Who is the fairest of them all?" And when she heard the answer – Snow White – she

burst into flames!

And Snow White and the prince lived happily ever after.